This book belongs to...

JUNGLE TALES
Super Snakes

Written by Ronne Randall
Illustrated by Jacqueline East

Bright ☆ Sparks

One morning, Seymour Snake's dad, Seymour Senior, said, "I have a surprise for you, son! Your cousin Sadie is coming to visit!"

"SSSensational!"

said Seymour.
"I haven't seen Sadie since we were little snakes. We used to have so much fun playing together. Now she can meet all my friends and join in our games!"

"Sadie may have changed a bit since you last saw her," said Seymour Senior. "She's been going to Madame Sylvia's Snake School."

"Oh, I'm sure she's still the same," said Seymour.

Later that day, Sadie came slithering down the path and Seymour wriggled up to greet her.

"Sadie!" cried Seymour. "It's so good to see you!"

"It's super to see you, too, Seymour," said Sadie.

"Come and meet my friends!" Seymour said eagerly. "You can play games with us, and…"

"Oh, I don't play games anymore," Sadie interrupted. "Madame Sylvia says it's not what good snakes should do. She always says, 'A well-behaved snake may slither and glide and wriggle and slide, but we DON'T swing or sway, or climb or play!'"

"You mean you don't climb trees?" asked Seymour.

"Certainly not!" said Sadie.

Seymour was shocked. "And you don't swing from branches?" he asked.

"Gracious, no!" replied Sadie.

"Well, will you at least come and meet my friends?" Seymour asked hopefully.

"Oh, yesss," said Sadie. "It would be rude not to!"

"HEY, SEYMOUR!" shouted Maxine Monkey. "Come and play Coconut Catch with Mickey and me!"

"Sure, guys!" said Seymour.

"By the way, this is my cousin Sadie."

"HI, SADIE!" shouted Mickey. Maxine and Mickey always shouted! "You can come and play, too."

"No, thank you," said Sadie. "I'll just watch. I don't swing or sway, or climb or play."

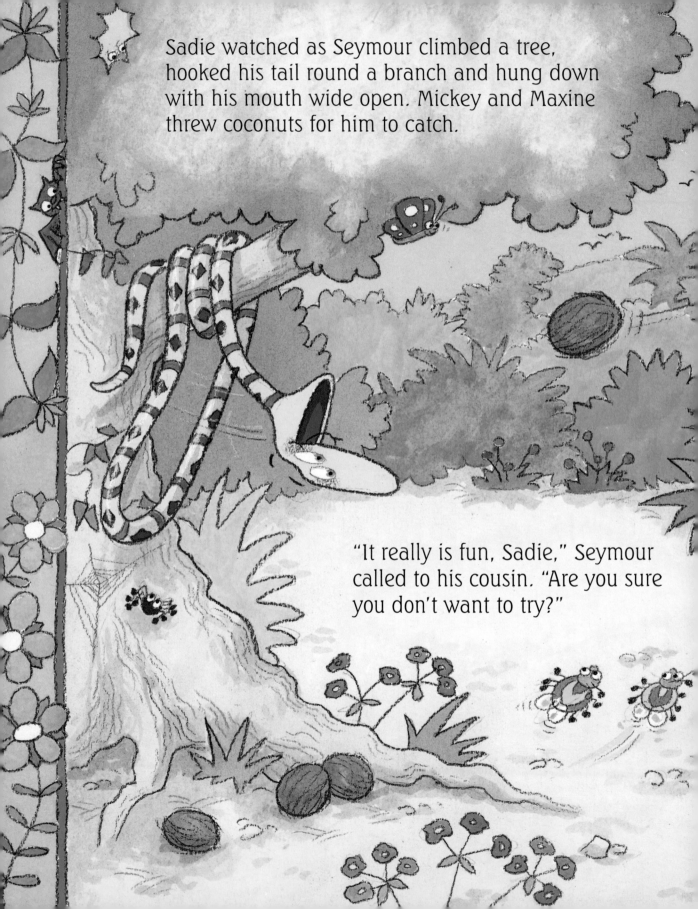

Sadie watched as Seymour climbed a tree, hooked his tail round a branch and hung down with his mouth wide open. Mickey and Maxine threw coconuts for him to catch.

"It really is fun, Sadie," Seymour called to his cousin. "Are you sure you don't want to try?"

"It looks interesting," Sadie admitted, "but I don't think so. Thank you anyway."

Seymour and the monkeys were just finishing their game, when Penelope Parrot arrived. After Seymour had introduced her to Sadie, Penelope asked him if he would help her practise her stunt flying.

"Sure, Penelope!"

said Seymour and he wound himself round the branch to make two loops.

WHOOOSH!

Penelope zoomed through one loop, swung round and ZOOMED back through the other.

"Tee-hee," giggled Seymour. "Your feathers tickle, Penelope! You really should try this, Sadie," he called to his cousin on the ground. "It's so much fun!"

Sadie hesitated. "Er, maybe some other time," she said, at last.

Seymour spent hours hanging and swinging and climbing— he even climbed to the very top of a tree to talk to Jeremy Giraffe.

Each time, Seymour invited Sadie to join him. And each time, Sadie looked more tempted – but she always said the same thing; "I mustn't swing or sway, or climb or play."

Later that day, Seymour spoke to his dad.

"I'm sure Sadie wants to play with me and my friends," he said. "But she insists on only watching. How can I get her to join in?"

"The only way," said Seymour Senior, "is to get Sadie to see for herself how much fun swinging and climbing can be."

Suddenly, Seymour had an idea.

"Thanks, Dad," he said. "That's just what I'll do! See you later!"

"Where are you going, Seymour?" asked his dad.

"I've got to talk to some of my friends," said Seymour. "I'll be back soon." And he slithered swiftly away down the path.

The next morning, Sadie was showing Seymour how smoothly she could slide and how gracefully she could glide, when suddenly there was a cry of

"OH, NO!"

Sadie slithered quickly ahead, only to find Ellen, Emma and Eric Elephant, staring up into the branches of a tree. They all looked very upset.

"What's wrong?" Sadie asked.

"We were playing Fling the Melon," said Ellen, "and I flung the melon so high, that it got stuck in the tree. Our trunks aren't long enough to reach it!"

"Oh, dear," said Sadie. "I'm sure Seymour will be happy to climb up and get it back for you. Won't you, Seymour? Seymour, where are you?"

Seymour had disappeared!

"Seymour must have gone home," said Emma. "Can't you help us, Sadie?"

"I'm sorry," said Sadie, "but I DON'T swing or sway..."

"...or climb or play," Emma finished. "We know about Madame Sylvia's rules. But surely Madame Sylvia must have taught you that it's important to help others," she said.

"Well," said Sadie, "she did teach us that we must never pass up an opportunity to do a good deed."

"And this would be such a good deed!" said Eric. "We would be so grateful!"

"All right," Sadie decided. "I'll do it!"

Up Sadie went, winding round the trunk, weaving her way up into the branches, until she reached the melon at the very top.

"Here it comes!" she shouted to the elephants, giving the melon a shove with her nose. It fell straight down into Ellen's waiting trunk.

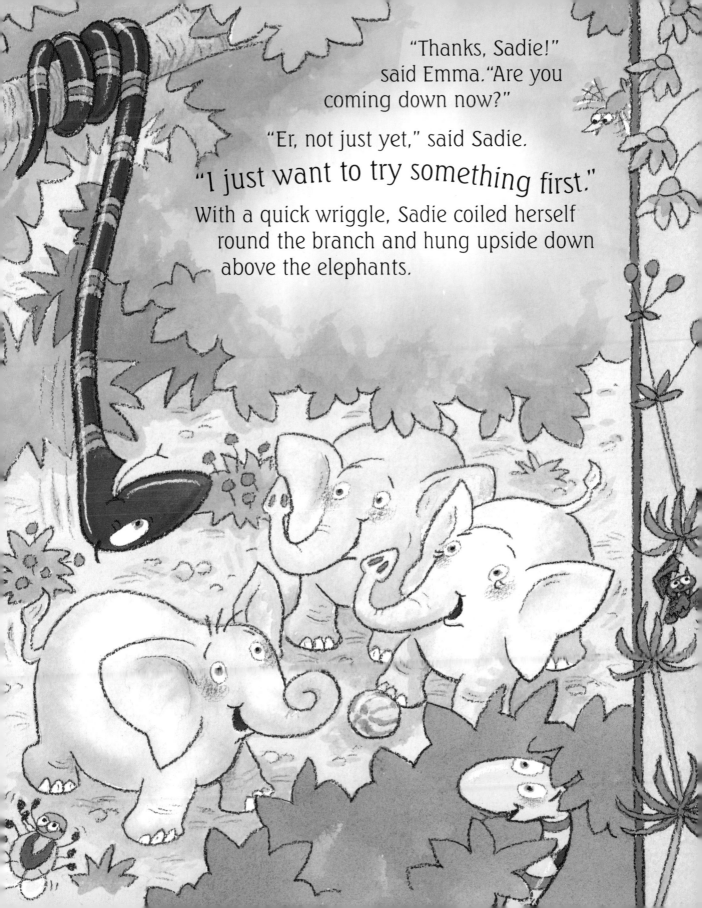

"Thanks, Sadie!"
said Emma. "Are you
coming down now?"

"Er, not just yet," said Sadie.
"I just want to try something first."
With a quick wriggle, Sadie coiled herself
round the branch and hung upside down
above the elephants.

"This is SSSUPER!"

Sadie shouted. "I haven't had so much fun in years! I wonder if I can – SWING?"

She swung herself over to another tree, "WHEEEEE!" she cried.

"I knew you'd like swinging and climbing if you just gave it a try," called Seymour, slithering out from where he'd been hiding.

"Come up here, Seymour!" Sadie called.
"We can swing and sway together."

"Here I come, Sadie," said Seymour, whizzing up the tree. "But what will you tell Madame Sylvia when you go back to school?"

"I'll just tell Madame Sylvia," said Sadie, "that we MUST climb and play, and swing and sway— ALL DAY!"

To which Seymour and his friends could only add a loud

"Hip-hip-HOORAY!"

The End

This is a Bright Sparks Book
First published in 2001
BRIGHT SPARKS, Queen Street House, 4 Queen Street, Bath BA1 1HE, UK

Copyright © PARRAGON 2001

Created and produced by THE COMPLETE WORKS,
St. Mary's Road, Royal Leamington Spa, Warwickshire CV31 1JP, UK

Printed in China

ISBN 1-84250-219-0